beyond
the horizon
beyond

beyond
the horizon
beyond

haiku and haibun

KALA RAMESH

Foreword by BILL KENNEY
Artwork by PRABHA MALLYA

beyond
the horizon
beyond

First Edition - August 2017

© Author

Published by:
Vishwakarma Publications
283, Budhwar Peth, Near City Post, Pune - 411002.
Phone No: (020) 20261157 / 24448989
Email: info@vpindia.co.in / Website: www.vpindia.co.in

Cover design by Prabha Mallya

Illustrations and cover art © Prabha Mallya

Typeset and Layout by Chaitali Nachnekar - Vishwakarma Publications

for
appa, akka,
& geeta,

> road trip -
>   the tree moves
> into the past
> touching memories

for
athira,

> I songwhisper
> my grandchild to sleep
> mango moon

beyond
the horizon
beyond …
waves of unknown oceans
inside this conch shell

CONTENTS

Illustrations by Prabha Mallya

The Moving Finger writes; and, having writ,
Moves on: nor all thy Piety nor Wit
Shall lure it back to cancel half a Line,
Nor all thy Tears wash out a Word of it.

— Omar Khayyam. [1]

Trees are poems the earth writes upon the sky,
We fell them down and turn them into paper,
That we may record our emptiness.

— Kahlil Gibran. [2]

FOREWORD

The Beginning of a Journey

What a wonderful gift Kala Ramesh gives us in *Beyond the Horizon Beyond,* a comprehensive collection of her haiku. In these poems, Kala inhabits and transcends two ancient traditions: from Japan, the tradition of haiku, within which Kala, true to the evolutionary dynamic of the form, moves with a complete imaginative and creative freedom; and from her native India, the deep resources of thought and spirituality that inform and complicate her modernity. In developing the themes drawn from these rich traditions and from her personal experience as a woman of her time (our time), Kala finds in English, her second language, an instrument of rare aesthetic beauty and expressive force.

The name "Kala" is derived from a Sanskrit word meaning "art," and it is the voice of an artist that we hear in these haiku. Trained in both instrumental and vocal traditions of Indian classical music, she brings to haiku a musician's sensibility, exquisitely attuned to the interplay of sounds, from the natural world and from the human. Most of us think we know the sound of a wolf's howl, but listen to what Kala hears:

night songs
gathering oneness
a wolf's howl

The middle line ("gathering oneness") looks both before and after

night songs
gathering oneness

but also

gathering oneness
a wolf's howl

Dualities (active/passive, subject/object, many/one) dissolve in a oneness that is nowhere and everywhere. The oneness the night songs gather includes the wolf's howl, as the oneness gathered in the wolf's howl includes the night songs. I'm not sure if you have to be a musician to hear what Kala hears. But I'm sure you have to be a poet.

What may be the role of the human voice in the oneness Kala celebrates? Does the voice of the muezzin in this haiku disturb the unity — seen now, and felt, rather than heard — of mountain and sky, or does it rather intensify our sense of oneness?

after sunset
mountains become the sky
a muezzin's call

"become" is, along with its variant forms, a key word in Kala's art. And here its appearance in the simple present tense introduces a teasing ambiguity:

> after sunset
> mountains become the sky

Is this the observation of a particular moment (this sunset) or a generalization about a recurrent phenomenon (sunsets in general)? The answer is found in line 3: the muezzin's call places us in the immediate present, a moment that unites the natural and the human, the physical and the spiritual (and, incidentally, the particular and the universal). Again, a oneness is asserted, a oneness seen as process, not product. "become" is the pivotal word. Everything that is (sunset, mountains, sky, the muezzin's call, and the moment of their gathering to oneness) is becoming.

And if we seek the source of this becoming, what do we find?

> everything
> comes from the unborn ...
> spring song

All that we know ("everything") comes from what is not ("un-"), but what is not is not mere negation; it is, rather, not yet ("un*born*"). Again the poet evades our categories, distinctions, definitions, bringing us to that moment in which all the things we know and do and are gathered to oneness.

The music that is in Kala's poetry is grounded in that rhythm of one/many, nothing/everything, nature/humanity, above/below. Thus, while she escapes our categories, it is not to descend into formlessness. Hear how her poet's art brings our sense of unlimited wonder into focus:

fireflies circling beyond circles the silence

Those of us who know fireflies will immediately recognize that circling. We see it, even as we know that it occurs, ultimately, not in the fireflies that are observed, but in the mind of the observer. (Compared to a circle, the movement of the fireflies is much more irregular, imperfect; that is its perfection.) It's the mind that "closes" the circle, but, the circle turns out not to be closed. It leads us beyond itself — indeed, "beyond circles." We arrive, inevitably, at "silence." But not permanently. This is a haiku, a "one-breath" poem, focusing on the all-at-onceness that is a moment. As we arrive at silence, the fireflies are still circling ...

It should be clear by now that the musicality of Kala's haiku is not merely a matter of its themes. Read any of these poems (all of them, indeed) aloud, and savor the melody of their becoming. In "fireflies" hear the sibilance ("circling ... circles ... silence"); catch the vowel rhyme that links the last word ("silence") to the first ("fireflies"); and listen for the way the word at the poem's center ("beyond," syllables 5-6 of an 11-syllable haiku), sharing no sound qualities with the rest, brings all into oneness.

We have been noting some of the ways Kala's background in music plays out in her haiku. But clearly the sense of sight plays a role in no way inferior to that of sound. It's no surprise, then, to learn that Kala's experience in the arts extends to the visual;

she has worked in watercolors and oils, even trying her hand, as she puts it, at portrait painting. Having walked with Kala through an American museum, I can personally attest to her fine visual intelligence.

Kala is in fact familiar with many of the arts of her native India, especially its great traditions of dance and drama. She has a sophisticated grasp of Indian aesthetics, and her work, as my remarks have already suggested, reflects her exposure to the Hindu philosophical exploration of Advaita, or non-duality. To Kala, all these modes of art and thought feed into one another, enriching the root of creativity. Always, the many resolve themselves into the one.

And all Kala's many interests and studies resolve themselves in Kala: Haiku poet? Indian poet? Woman poet? A phenomenal poet, surely, ever absorbing and moving beyond what she finds in haiku, in art, in philosophy, in life. Travel with her as she takes us beyond the horizon beyond.

Bill Kenney
Whitestone NY USA
20 May 2017

Thirty spokes share the wheel's hub;
It is the centre hole that makes it useful.
Shape clay into a vessel;
It is the space within that makes it useful.

— Tao Te Ching of Lao Tzu. [3]

PREFACE

This is the journey of my cultural memory. The five elements — ether, air, fire, water and earth, known as 'Panchabhutas' — have always fascinated me. In Sanskrit, 'pancha' means five and 'bhutas' are the natural elements. As I began to delve deeper into the ancient texts, I found that each of these elements was related to one particular sense.

Ether (akash) is associated with *sound*. Air (vayu) with *sound and touch*. Fire (agni) with *sound, touch and sight*. Water (jalam) with *sound, touch, sight and taste;* and finally, Earth (prithvi) is associated with *sound, touch, sight, taste and smell*. I got goosebumps when I read this the first time. It seemed to fit haiku so well and it gave me a grip over the way both my interior and exterior worlds worked in my writing.

Since haiku is so closely associated with seasonal references, the association of the five elements with the five senses greatly interested me. I found that Ayurveda, a system of medicine with historical roots in India, followed these five elements in its line of treatment. Vastu Shastra, which is a traditional Indian system of architecture and the science of designing one's house in accordance with nature, is also based on these five elements.

Excited, I decided to weave these five elements through my haiku, taking into consideration the nuances and extension of the five senses as perceived in our ancient texts.

Thus we have:

> Ether (Akash): associated with space, knowledge, intuition, dignity, oneness, trust, creativity and *sound*.

> Air (Vayu): associated with wind, breeze, lightness, birds, feathers, inhalation, exhalation, lungs, compassion and *touch*.

> Fire (Agni): associated with colours orange, red, yellow, vibrancy, brightness, warmth, wisdom, activity, destruction, ash, power and *sight*.

> Water (Jalam): associated with touch, hearing, saltiness, sight, joy, well-being, flexibility, flooding, finding one's level, clouds, fog, mist, snow and *taste*.

> Earth (Prithvi): associated with hearing, touch, sight, taste, sweetness, sourness, stability, support, astringency, shadow, light, shade, famine, family ties, birth, death and *smell*.

Being a student of classical vocal music, I was exposed to Kabir, a 15th-century Indian mystic-poet-saint, and I was greatly intrigued by his direct reproach to superstition and the upside-down language (known as *ulatbamsi*—"poems with outrageous, nonsensical, sometimes shocking imagery," according to Linda Hess) that is beautifully interwoven into many of his poems.

He also explored tantric practices and made reference to our outer and inner lives. In one of his poems, he talks about the ten doors human beings have:

> You go around
> bent! bent! bent!
> Your ten doors are full of hell, you smell
> like a fleet of scents,
> your cracked eyes don't see the heart,
> you haven't an ounce of sense.
> Drunk with anger, hunger, sex,
> you drown without water.

The Bijak of Kabir
Translated by Linda Hess and Shukdev Singh. [4]

For years, I could never understand Kabir's allusion to the ten doors ... but all of a sudden, after I came into haiku, these ten doors made a connection, setting off a spark of consciousness in my thinking. I almost experienced a satori. My interpretation of Kabir's ten doors, as you would expect, is connected to the five senses — two doors for sight (eyes), two doors for hearing (ears), two doors for smell (nostrils), one door for taste (mouth) and three doors for touch (anus, urethra and genitals). As haiku poets, we know there's constant traffic going in and out of these ten doors ... and we are gifted with a pulsating consciousness registering these blatant, clear-cut feelings that constantly enter our minds through the ten doors. These openings are our doors to the outside world, connecting the 'panchabhutas' to the five senses as explained above.

My title, *'beyond the horizon beyond,'* suggests both conclusion and continuity. A few years ago, I attended a one-month course on film appreciation at the Film and Television Institute of India, to study how directors use the 'cut,' called 'kire,' which is the essential element that makes the haiku art form different. While reading about 'Noh' drama, I came across the term 'kire-tsuzuki' or 'cut-continuity.' The commonest example of this is the pause between every exhalation of air from the lungs and the next inhalation. Another lovely example is our walk - we move one leg, cut the movement and move the other leg - the two actions together get us moving; there is both a cut and a continuation. The title embodies and exemplifies this idea of both conclusion and continuity. The continuation leads one to 'Zoka,' the creative force of nature, a Japanese concept used in haiku. In Sanskrit, we call this 'Prakriti.' Prakriti is described in the *Bhagavad Gita* as the 'primal motive force.'

The title, *'beyond the horizon beyond,'* also embodies the void around things, an uncluttered feeling in our minds and our surroundings. The nearer you get to a horizon the farther it moves away. Once you go 'beyond' there is no 'beyond.' Beyond the horizon there is only 'Śhūnyatā' — the void that resonates with the sound of positive energy — 'Omkara.' In the silence between notes, between words, between lines, the emotional quotient that arises is 'rasa,' as we say in India — that which gives poetry, music, dance or any other art form greater depth and resonance. It is something that cannot be described in words, because it has taken us to a sublime plane where all sounds have dropped away.

How closely these thoughts connect with my understanding of haiku, for haiku revolves around the Japanese aesthetic concept known as 'ma' (pronounced as 'mah'). I can't do better than quote from an interview with Hasegawa Kai in the Spring 2009 issue of *Simply Haiku*.

> "In other words, juxtaposition is a technique for creating 'ma' in haiku. A more realistic problem for discussion is that of ma. This Japanese word can have a spatial meaning, as in 'empty space' or 'blank space,' a temporal meaning (silence), a psychological meaning, and so on. Ma is at work in various areas of life and culture in Japan. Without doubt, Japanese culture is a culture of ma. This is the case with haiku as well. The "cutting" (kire) of haiku is there to create ma, and that ma is more eloquent than words. That is because even though a superior haiku may appear to be simply describing a 'thing,' the working of ma conveys feeling (kokoro)."

'beyond the horizon beyond' includes haibun as well as haiku. What is haibun if not an extension of a haiku that gives us more space to carry a story forward? The 'link and shift' that we employ between the prose and the haiku is a precious gift from the Japanese that can be used extensively in all art forms.

Nobuyuki Yuasa says, "In good haibun, the prose deepens the understanding of the poetry, and the poetry gives greater energy to the prose. The relationship is like that between the moon and the earth: each makes the other more beautiful." (*Blithe Spirit,* Sept 2000).

It is amazing to see the reach of human thought and cultures, over hills and seas, as our quest to understand the 'unknown' continues ... beyond the horizon beyond.

Kala Ramesh
Pune, India
17 May 2017

ACKNOWLEDGEMENTS

All of the haiku and haibun presented here were first published in well-known journals including *Acorn, A Hundred Gourds, Asahi Shimbun Newspaper Japan, Akita International Haiku Network, Ambrosia Journal of Fine Haiku, Bones, Bottle Rockets, Blithe Spirit: British Haiku Society, Cattails, Chrysanthemum, Colorado Boulevard.net, Contemporary Haibun Online, Frameless Sky, Frogpond, Frozen Butterfly, Genjuan Haibun Contest, Golden Triangle, Indi Kukai, Haibun Today, Haiku 21, Haiku Chronicles, Haiku Harvest, Haiku News, Haiku North America Anthology 2015 & 17, Haiku Reality, Haiku in English: First Hundred Years, Haiku Prix, Hedgerow, Issa's Untidy Hut, is/let, Katha, Kokako, Kernels' Online, Kyoto Journal, Lynx, Lakeview International Journal of Literature and Arts, Mann Library's Daily Haiku: Cornell University Library, Magnapoets, Mainichi Daily News, Mayfly, Modern Haiku, Moonset - the Newspaper, Muse India, Muttering Silence, Narrow Road, Narthaki.com, Notes From the Gean, one-line twos, One Over the Eighth, Potpourri Haiku Desk Calendar, Presence Haiku Journal, Prune Juice, Red Moon Press, Roadrunner, Samobor Croatia, Shamrock, Shadow Poetry, Shiki Monthly Kukai, Shreve Memorial Library's Electronic Poetry Network, Pune 365, Simply Haiku, Sketchbook, Snapshot*

Press, Sonic Boom, South by Southwest, Stylus, Tempslibres, Tinywords, The Asahi Shimbun, The Heron's Nest, 3 Lights Gallery, Trilopia, Under the Basho, Upstate Dim Sum, Wednesday Haiku, Whirligig, Whispers, Wild Plum, The Haiku Foundation, The Hindu, The Living Haiku Anthology, and *The World Haiku Review.* I thank each and every editor for encouraging me to find my voice; without that encouragement, this body of work would not exist.

I would like to express my deepest gratitude to Bill Kenney for his heartwarming 'Foreword,' and to Richard Gilbert for his lovely comment on my haiku; my admiration and thanks to Prabha Mallya for all the artwork; and my deepest gratitude to my colleagues, Shloka Shankar, Sanjuktaa Asopa and Jayashree Maniyal who helped me get some sense of proportion in my selection process, although of course I added my favourites. Thanks to my dear friend, Jenny Angyal, for her mastery over editing, proofreading and for all the beautiful suggestions she gave, which I gratefully accepted; and to Lorin Ford, Carole MacRury, Francine Banwarth, Melissa Allen and Abigail Friedman for their valuable input regarding the preface and the poems. Thanks also to young Dishika Iyer for her help.

To my AHA forum friends, starting with the late Jane Reichhold, my IN Haiku family and to all the Indian haiku poets who write in English and other regional languages, a Himalayan-sized 'thank you' for your companionship and encouragement through the years.

My special thanks to Geeta Dharmarajan and Katha.org for all the encouragement they have given to haiku. I thank Vishal Soni and Chaitali Nachnekar of Vishwakarma Publications for publishing this book. My deep gratitude to my students who attended the various workshops I've been conducting for the past ten years, for they have helped me to look deeper into my knowledge of haiku, senryu, tanka, haibun, tanka prose and renku ... to look beyond rules and beyond words. My special thanks to my seniors, Dr Angelee Deodhar, Dr Johannes Manjrekar and K. Ramesh, and to my music guru, Smt. Shubhada Chirmulay for all the encouragement they have given me.

To my parents, Dr N. Krishnaswamy and Smt. Kalyani Krishnaswamy — how can I ever find words to thank them, for everything I am today is because of what they have given me. My appreciation and thanks to my siblings and my children for always being there to encourage and applaud as I began to walk the haiku path.

I remain,
greatly indebted ...

Kala Ramesh
May 2017

We are animal in our blood and in our skin. We were not born for pavements and escalators, but for thunder and mud.

— Jay Griffiths. [5]

HAIKU

Earth : PRITHVI

swollen buds
the fragrance becoming
a child's breath

a cow emerges —
the dry weeds knotted
on her horns

his outstretched hand
   pins that perfect note ...
nirguni bhajan

for Kumar Gandharva

deep in raga
   sudden applause
startles the singer

evening concert
her diamond nose pin shines
at every nuance

for M. S. Subbulakshmi

spotlight ...
from within he draws
a lilting step

for Kelucharan Mohapatra

Devi temple ...
along with the ants
I enter barefoot

abhinaya ... *
her face in liquid gold
of the setting sun

body and facial expression

the dais —
her eyes speak the language
I understand

a bamboo flute sounds   on the path
flowers strewn   as I walk past

a zip haiku for John Carley,
creator of the form

morning raga ...
a honeybee attempts
to waken the bud

her nipples through the t-shirt this self-awareness

spring mela ...
after much haggling, I win
the laughing Buddha

flies
even inside the temple
Issa

a breathtaking view now a dot :: on the map

the pause
in a dragonfly's glide —
noon shadows

waiting room
a spider hangs
on silence

rainforest
    the lives
I step on

the lie betrayed a hundredfold cracked mirror mirror

a falling blossom …
the breath between what was
and what will be

garden party
father talks to his plants
before guests arrive

a leaf
caught by the boulder
   I pause
      the ahimsa's way

communal riot ...
the fog slowly releases
  the morning quiet

weathered field —
waiting for the buds to bloom
not by name

kalachakra ...
the shadow of a moth
circling the hour

unvoiced
arguments at dinner
the sound of cutlery

beach dinner
the papad in her hand
dwarfs the moon

a world beyond the word I scribble my name

daylily
worries drag on
into the night

the weight
weighs itself out ...
falling leaves

mortuary
even after death
we're tagged

the land
  rivered no more
arrowroot fields

withering blossom —
        clay takes shape
on the potter's wheel

CONGRATULATIONS
you've won $5,000,000.00 USD:
I count the zeros

my mind dreams dreams pillows let go

window shopping ...
on a headless mannequin
my face appears

forest walk —
a spider's shadow
climbs the tree

mountain shadow robs the tree of its

my second
green mango of the day
first trimester

breastfeeding ...
was the fragrance of champa
also born of a dream

every resemblance
in their newborn
gets promptly claimed

parijaat blossom ...
as kids, we shook the tree
for raindrops

love scene
    my daughter
drops the remote

male gaze :: the female in me squares up her arms

a tale
behind each bit o' bling
red light district

wild violets ...
     he finally agrees
to the path I took

in his roomy absence I feel the walls

winter rain
colder than ever
this bowl of rice

autumn leaves am I the one I am

longer than the leaf month nostalgia

double rainbow
the day I discovered
my vagina

raga kalyaan
the pumpkin gourd
   yields an autumn lyric

winter loneliness
   sittingtogether
in our own thoughts

winter dusk morphing into a den of old songs

sanctum sanctorum
      the gods
in darkness

sandcastle
      my child in
his own world

Saturday night dinner
the guests all-consumed
with their own stories

foreign country
the maid and I
keep smiling

coffee lounge
we act out each other's
bored look

sunset ...
the cuckoo repeats
his morning song

autumn path
where do cuckoos hide
their songs

hoping he removes
my tooth, the whole tooth
and nothin' but the tooth

bronze swan
the paper weight holds
my thoughts

black ants all over the mud hill in undulation

Saturday night dinner
           one after another
his jokes

bed time
she asks if her rag doll
can stay up late

the band-aid covering a band-aid mother's kiss

paddy fields
our car passes
a milestone

home-ripened mangoes
I hear my grandmother's voice
in my mother's

falling leaves ...
if only sorrow could be
contained in a palm

winter loneliness
the sofa she vacates
holds her shape

not a soul ...
the moon has moved
from my window

who bears
the weight of separation
fallen blossom

a cuckoo sings
the darkness of leaves
before dawn

cotton candy
the sun-drenched waves
of childhood laughter

narrow road
the clash of umbrellas
as we near the Buddha

the threshold I
    falter on autumn's
        pebbled path

incomplete beings
you and I
complete the city

my hometown
a strong fragrance
of mango dawn

toe rings tinkle amma's autumn pace

I walk farther
into the womb of time:
Mohenjo-daro

withered field —
slowly coming to terms
with my aborted child

autumn lyrics
father talks about life
beyond death

the magician
              surprised
by his own magic

at the premiere
a soprano's bosom fills
the spotlight

rewriting a cheque
once again
my signature goes awry

dense fog ...
  I dream walk
my sense of I

the knife sharpener
on his bicycle —
      falling leaves

escaping
rules and laws
I sneak in

painting class
children colour each other
into laughter

autumn trees —
passengers in the train
behind their newspapers

morning raga
yesterday's buds
in full bloom

her plait in step with her hips a string of jasmine

when the latest fashion
least interests you,
you begin to show your age

creaksong

one word haiku: for autumn

an ant an ant a sugargrain many times their weight

harvesting grapes ...
the season slips through
her fingers

an old woman
straightens her shadow
deep autumn

burning ghat ...
   from the depths of grief
my friend's off-key tune

autumn nightfall ...
without any fuss the end
of a yellow leaf

Water : JALAM

sans shore
horizon or sky: I am
a waterlily

after Monet's 'Water Lilies' at L'Orangerie

crossing river boulders
    the moon becomes whole again

                    fish   fish
mountain stream   popping

liquid sky ...
a steel bucket hits
the well water

she draws a bucket her face from the well

monsoon beat
the shimmering length
of a coconut tree

darkening sky
the river gives no reason
for its song

fish kill
they decide against
children

the iceberg of thought as I begin to voice my mind

oceans with names —
        waves leaping over
one another

looking
for a river that is no more
ancestral home

summer thunder ...
stepping out with bare feet
my soul

leaves and rain:
my umbrella flips
into a bowl

water crowns
the spontaneous rise
of small desires

monsoon!
the road home
rushing to meet me

in the darkness
of the womb, a life swims
into my life

the river carries the raga of a thousand moons

muggy weather
      I space out
my poems

father's day
we order our meal
with less salt

snowballs
I become the grandchild
I'm waiting for

crashing sea waves rockcradled into silence

sunset
I walk my shadow
to the sea

a village
far below, as fog lifts ...
the blue mountains

on the lake
skimming stones, I am
where I am

chakraasana *
I slip
on my sweat

wheel pose in yoga

the struggle to get a lily to stay in water after all

after Nick Virgilio's 'lily' haiku

the ocean in a raindrop inside my womb a heart

with droplets life giving first breast-feed

baby tortoise
how old
is ancient

summer moon
a wave's white foam
glazes the rock

beach sands ...
beyond the sway of her hips
the surging sea

the pause
he takes on his flute —
spring rain

white water rafting
        we spin around
our laughter

the waterfall rock tumbling speckled rhythms

gusty storm —
the weathercock tilts
its nose up

rowing
      the fog
into the fog

my monsoon sale bargains —
all through the year
his critique

she brings in
the first rain on little feet ...
evening prayers

she looks down
from the ninth floor apartment:
umbrellas with legs

thin mist ...
a frothy wave advances
the horizon

autumn lake
a speedboat sounding
the curve

a sacrificial goat
bleeds
      the Kali temple
at the rivulet

waterfall
        I walk
the sound

temple bells
the isolated raindrops
on my umbrella

thunderclap —
the darkening sky splits
into liquid night

wild bamboo
the pencilled darkness
shimmers in rain

cyclone —
she holds the umbrella
the sari holds her

midnight jetty
the sound of water
slapping water

an hour slips by
threading your absence
the rain

water buffaloes —
shoreline shadows pleat
the monsoon lake

paper moon ...
  a cliff-diver folds
in the setting sun

water circles becoming wide the frog's next leap

I am
what I make of dreams
        a dewdrop
holds the moon

winter rain
      a cadence
to our love making

a nakedness
the morning after
cyclonic rains

a sudden fish-like dart my womb tilts in balance

bus ride in monsoon
a snoring man's head bounces
at the pothole

low tide
the silence of a wave
wets my mind

spring rain ...
halfway through my meal
a scoop of loneliness

amavasya *
the river flows on sounds
    the river makes

       * *a no-moon night*

stable river banks ...
our memory of hopscotch
under shade trees

wooden bridge ...
a maple leaf settles
on its reflection

liquid twilight
the tilt of a water pot
on her hip

waterfall ...
do darting birds
tickle it?

midnight raga
the river
lost

village talk ...
the breadth of paddy fields
as monsoon delays

distant thunder
                this fear
the colour of my walls

sultry evening
   the sound of rain
on banana leaves

jasmine rain ...
burrowing into the distant
sand bed of my past

temple elephant —
a mahout rides into
the gathering mist

cyclonic rains
coconut leaves dip
into streetlights

the quickening beat
of raindrops on autumn leaves —
I begin to hum

the ease of a ballpoint my life on the move

kingfishers pick
the tumbling river notes ...
evening raga

I dip my feet
in a river the river
joins the sea

Fire : AGNI

temple redone
    Kali's tongue
not so red

Diwali night
    the diya *
lights up her face

    * *an earthen oil lamp*

his eyes speak
  before his tongue
one more lie

this forest fire shocks the sun ghost white

London morning dew —
fumes through my nostrils and mouth
like an Eastern dragon

muggy shed ...
a cow's skin quivers
the flies away

blistering heat
a storytelling of ravens
on the riverbed

the first drizzle
streaks the brick wall
... sizzling heat

ice cream season
  I must have been
a dog once

firefly!
  hitching a ride
on its own light

stinging nettles
I still recall
his words

bone density ...
the branch crumbles
after the forest fire

expressway ...
the winter sun we raced
now at my window

roadside laughter ...
a flipped glass marble catches
the autumn sunlight

a dream light through this morning's glasswing

long day
a lizard up the brick wall
   a limb
      at a time

more and more the rumour spreading forest fire

first cut!
a watermelon seller
bites into his profit

crackling bonfire my days are still interesting

steaming rice
served on banana leaves ...
he loosens his tie

the voice
beyond the gaslight's reach
village play

fallen blossom
the silent farewell
deepens the sunset

slipping in
beneath the kitchen door
— first sunlight

dense fog
the train evaporates
into a distant horn

temple gate:
the wind gets in faster
than the devotees

thunder coming downhill the sound of glass bangles

summer sky
temple doves somersault
into wingsong

autumn dusk
the leaves rustle
on a bass note

the whistling comet on an octave drop

soap bubbles
　　how softly mother
bursts into laughter

trying out hearing aids
　　　　she calls out
　　her own name

into the night a cuckoo returns the call

slicing wind
the skylark alone
knows the pull

her hips
as she takes the curve ...
ice skating

the next step I leave behind a bush warbler's song

twilight trees
birds go in and out
of song

taking flight —
a butterfly flicks off
its shadow

temple arch
a child on her appa's shoulders
rings the bell

bulbul
    the wind
owns the song

spring breeze —
    I catch the tune
she leaves behind

the resonant call
from a sparrow's tiny lungs
— basant *

basant is a spring raga

on a leaf an inchworm prowls an inch of air

a thousand flutes
from the bamboo forest
summer's end

gentle breeze —
the touch of his kurta
on my skin

joggers' park
the wind circling leaves
circling the wind

boxed in I search for a key to open spaces I dream of

horror movie
my sister screams between
her fingers

mild breeze breadth of the wheat field's whisper

a rocking chair
on the uneven floor ...
winter quiet

waiting for his call
the pendulum swings
into New Year

sleepless ...
a swaying web catches
and loses the light

the wind howling horizon on a wave

sports stadium
she throws the keys perfectly
into his hands

an untouchable
        we share
the street air

the pecking
amongst a rush of wings
... rice sparrows

kite contest
    the rise and fall
of oos and aahs

the sari slides
down her shoulder
spring breeze

my thoughts
nudge each other ...
bumping bees

on the wings
of a butterfly ... the orange
I carry home

bearded vulture —
   the wingspan extends
      mountain to mountain

a yellow breeze
ruffles the hill's outline
summer grass

blossoms ...
    the dog leap-curves
        towards the frisbee

scrambling for words —
      a birdsong in flight
deep in me

Ether : AKASH

morning prayers
the rising sun between
my hands

where forest meets water fireflies explode the night

heaven's river from where to where

the year passes ...
longing for cranes
to colour the sky

Gita chanting
... birds become
the ellipsis

a mango plucked
    an empty space   to the sky

daybreak —
stars abandon the moon

running downhill
    I fall through
        the autumn sky

dhyaan *
a cuckoo's song
fills the void

meditation in Sanskrit

tower of silence
        the cawing of
a hundred crows, not one
vulture

how little
I know of bird calls
distant thunder

the attic ...
that old Murphy radio
father talked about

a dragonfly punctuating silence

after sunset
mountains become the sky
a muezzin's call

the gibbous moon a one-breast enticer amongst stars

to the terrace
whistling :: breathless
the milky way

honeycomb
I search for those spaces
within me

morning star
the way I hold on
to dreams

Gurbani temple music
    the rhythm of heaven
        joins in as thunder

I suck in
the noodle till it ends ...
milky way

waiting
   for a bengal tiger
I sense the power
of silence

everything
comes from the unborn ...
spring song

full car park
the winter moon
at every turn

daybreak
the valley brimful
of blue sky

my fear ...
   the darkness
between stars

Gita recital
as each stanza ends
the bell

leaf tip
an inchworm's search
for a landing

eagles a mere speck
sapaat taans begin their climb *
morning concert

tree crickets
    all at once
the night sky

* Sapaat taans are straight fast passages sung with the tabla (drums).
Often musicians cover all three octaves.

the space between stars mymindclutter

a lotus
    out of the muck
the flowering
within

mountain bridge
    I pass through
the cloud

dark forest the isness in *is*

darkness at its deepest pitch cicadas hold their note

still water ...
that longing to be
a bird in the cloud

desert sands ...
I enter the whole
of nothingness

Tibetan bowl
with a wooden stick
I circle Aum

night songs
gathering oneness
a wolf's howl

sleepless night
but does my dog have
Buddha nature

who am I *
night and day merge
in twilight

   * *after Ramana Maharshi*

a story from a seed   blossoming
 at the end   Śhūnyatā

the sky
on a morning lake ...
that perfect lotus

HAIBUN
the story continues

The Rajkumari

During our summer vacation, for forty-five straight days we jumped around, playing a different game each morning, afternoon and evening. Aeroplane hopscotch was a favourite. Long skirts held high to avoid erasing the chalk lines, we leaped with our legs spread wide to straddle the lines.

One afternoon, a soothsayer walked into our compound leading a young bull loaded with old clothes that people had given him. From the small drum-like instrument fitted into his palm came a constant sound: gudu gudu gudu. In Tamizh we called these people gudu gudu paandi.

He told my mother he was an expert fortune-teller, and we all showed him our palms. Being the youngest, I went last. I don't remember what he told my sisters, but I will never forget how he studied my palm and proclaimed, "You'll live like a princess." Only five-and-a-half, I spent the rest of my holidays dreaming that I was a Rajkumari (crown princess).

> soap bubbles ...
> when all the world
> was young

Bhoot
— The Ghost

Every night on the yet-to-be-tiled staircase, at the far corner of the landing, with hair flying all over, that out-of-this-world howl would lurch towards us. My eldest sister and I would go screaming down the few steps we had climbed ... and as usual my mother would shout at Giri, telling her to behave. Giri was our sister, the bold one! I was just six years old but I can still remember the cold, rough floor ...

an owl's screech
the seamless night
ripped in two

The Sutra

> sepals around a bud
> mountains guard
> the riversong

I would potter around as our gardener tended to each and every plant in the garden. He would gently loosen the soil with bare hands, saying "it has to breathe, just like you and me." I was eight years old then, and I remember Chinnappa.

Once when he was working with a hibiscus plant, I went running to fetch water. He stopped me. "No," he said, in his Tamizh dialect. "Let the soil and the plant breathe for some time, the water will only soak the soil and dampen their spirit." I laughed at the thought, and even repeated it to my parents later.

Once I dug a one-rupee coin out from my pocket and pretended I had found it in the soil, saying in a grand fashion, "it's for you, Chinnappa."

Long after he retired, his daughter called one day to say the doctors had given up on him, and that he mumbled about wanting to see our family.

> arterial roads
> a breathlessness
> in my heart

The River

Maya's mother had always been known to tell stories well; it was much, much later when we came to know she had a poet hidden in her. She loved telling us little anecdotes, adding an ear here or a nose there, as we say in Tamizh. When we asked her to repeat an old story, we would keenly watch how and where she added that extra something to make the story all sparkling new!

> a wanderer
> slipping out of the pond
> the moon

Maya often told me how she savoured these tales, hoping their interesting characters would surface in her dreams. She dreamed a lot and her elder sister, Kaveri, who had theories about dreams, stated firmly that "only creative people dream, and I've never, ever, had a dream."

Theirs was an ancestral house. Nearly a hundred years old, with the traditional columned courtyard in the centre, open to the sky. It was sheer space. From the front door to the backyard, the columns, windows, and doors were made from Burma teak. Everyone said the Burma teak was "solid," so Maya often rapped on the columns until her knuckles were sore and red. Maya remembered how they played aeroplane hopscotch in this courtyard, and how it morphed into their rain-dance arena too. And how, they slept on grass mats laid close to one another, blanketed by a starry night.

creaksong ...
autumn wind swinging
on the barnyard gate

Kulfiwala

On Saturday nights we wait
for that man on his old bicycle
his voice most peculiar
unmistakable even in my dreams

hearing him again tonight
my mouth begins to water —
breathing in, the scent runs a marathon
coming out through my skin

he opens a terracotta pot
from which he digs out
a small cylindrical aluminium cone

as each clamours to be the first
he gives that all knowing smile
as he hands me, the youngest of us all,
the first plate
made from areca leaves
with neatly sliced ice cream on it

I hold it precariously
not wanting to drop any of it
nor wanting to be the first to begin
for then I'll be the first to finish

and I will have to see my siblings
eat, lick and eat and ...
my eyes would refuse to look away

"Kulfiwala!" mother calls out
to give him the money
for our once-a-week sin
— an almond, cashew
and cardamom mix
of home-made ice cream
the bestest in the world

      the joy in her voice
      I remember as a child
      Mother's Day

            bronze temple bell
            the mingling undertones
            of myriad thoughts

Captured

Between here and the bank on the other side of the river, a catamaran bobs in the bright morning light. I can hear the water slapping its sides. We are on our summer vacation, on a road trip down South India. Our first halt is at Bhavani village, where my father has hired a small cottage. I'm sitting on the veranda facing a never-ending green rice field. A short distance away, the river meanders toward an ashram.

I'm twelve years old, just entering womanhood, sensing situations in a more intense way. My two elder sisters, always having done things together, have gone off, leaving me alone to my daydreams ... My younger brother is all curled up on the divan, with a Hardy Boys book, his latest craze.

I see Garuda, the giant eagle, sweep across the twilight skies. I build on the great epic — Ramayana — the story of Lord Rama and his consort Sita. In this dream, I'm the ever-gentle, beautiful Sita, the heroine, who is abducted by Ravana, the ten-headed demon king of Sri Lanka. Riding on his royal chariot, Ravana engages in a fierce battle with Garuda in the sky, as I struggle to get away from Ravana's grasp.

mango grove
pencils of rays streaming in
a n y w h i c h w a y

The Third Note

I was twelve years old when I first heard the musician, affectionately called Flute Maali, play. The concert hall was packed, the silence complete, as we waited for that first note.

> a firefly trails
>   the stillness
> of mountain treetops

It was a known fact that he often came onto the dais drunk. The flask from which he took frequent sips was rumoured to hold whiskey. Sometimes, he would arrive hours late, and after the long wait, it would be announced that the musician had actually arrived and would be on stage in a few moments.

At times, if the quality of the first note was not to his liking, his face would droop with disappointment and the audience would respond with a soft moan. Today, his bamboo flute perfectly touches the third note on the scale, the majestic Gandhar. Emotions leap in the silence after the note, as the musician gently coaxes the beauty of the raga into our very being.

> the sunflower faces the sun rises

Grandfather

On the radio, a film song from the 40's ...

Grandfather gets into one of his talking moods ... "Your grandmother — what a sweet woman she was, how pretty to look at — not the way these beauty queens look, huh? Tell me grandson — do you really like these girls so thin? Why do you smile? You think that beauty can be appreciated only by you young fellows?

"Madhubala*... did you know I had a picture of her in my cupboard, till your grandmother discovered it one day? 'What? You worm!' she screamed at me. I snatched the photo from her and tore it up. Later, I went into the bathroom and wept bitterly, because Madhubala had been with me through my college days and now she was no more."

> he begins to snore
> on whiffs of raat ki rani *
> ... night raga

Notes:
* *Madhubala was a renowned Hindi actress in the 40's.*
* *night jasmine*

Morning Fog

a replay
of the years gone by —
an old stage song

What a whirlwind ride it was while it lasted
Lasted, a mere six months or was it slightly longer
Longer, just as an orchid holds on to the last month to peer
into the next ...

early morning fog
                joggers
        run on air

The Smile

moonlight ...
on a roller-coaster ride
the sea-scented waves

High on a peak we stood, hand in hand. So easy, so effortless it seemed, to be in love, to be lovers, unaware that life's frictions were just around the corner.

It was just around the corner that I met you, that first time. Our eyes locked, a moment of awareness filled my being ... adjusting my sari, my hair, I see you smile ...

Your smile, how distant it seems now. If I were to see you now, would I even remember the feelings your smile roused in me, that day?

fireflies!
muted shades of emotions
crisscross

The Nuances

cavechested I feed you wanting to give everything I possess my child your first gulp I follow until it reaches your stomach almost a smile of satisfaction if giving is gaining a joy shared your heaving bosom

> preschool gate
> her face, in the space between
> farewells

Notes:
Beginning from the womb, the bond between the mother and her child-to-be, called 'vaatsalya', is the purest form of love, according to our ancient Sanskrit texts.

Aditya

— The Sun God

I get away from the crowd, on to the top of a hill. On the other side is the peacock valley, where I see retired men sitting in groups, chatting their idle hours away.

A young couple pass by me. Suddenly, she stops midway, pulling his sleeves, saying, "Look, look! How beautiful!" I see a copper-red plate swivelling as it slips downward. Sheer vibrancy envelops the entire lake below in burning oranges and reds. A sacred moment, this twilight, perfect because it's neither day nor night, neither light nor darkness and without a double, it has come to stay in my mind.

> string of jasmine
> her plait in step
> with her hips

The Fire at the End

What is it about the fire at the end of a rolled paper? A well-known Indian film director once said that it was this fire that helped him think.

Let's move our focus to this man sitting on the park bench, lighting his cigarette in a meticulous fashion, unknowingly taking his act to the level of a fine art. He could be slightly nervous, though, for there's a mild tremor in his hand. As the light falls on his face, the creases show up as distinctly as his pinched cheeks. He leans back on the hard cement bench. Three more puffs, the fourth and then slowly a long drawn out fifth. He calms down ... and seems to slip into a trance, the smoke curls into space.

> autumn chill
> the ashtray holds
> their conversation

Her eyes were a dark brown, unusual for a Tamizh girl ... Even now when he goes to Chennai, he unwittingly searches for her, as she was, so many years back — his mind refusing to see that she mightn't recognise him at all ... or might not want to.

Autumn's Depth

I hug Amma — her back has been hurting her, yet she smiles through the pain. I'm reminded of the red brick wall in our yard, now parched of rain, cracking under the Chennai summer.

When I was young, she always said that she would love to grow old gracefully. But now, I wonder, does it mean dyeing one's hair and having a face-lift to seem young, or does it mean going with the flow — ageing, like the stars in the sky — accepting that helping hand and holding on to the rails when climbing up the stairs?

> the huge bronze bell
> rings in autumn's depth ...
> hill temple

The Old Album

Her favourite things were the blue tickle frock, which had moon holes all around the waist, and the hole book, which she would rotate as far as it would go, hooked between her first finger and the thumb. She was very ticklish and anticipating one she would break into peals of laughter. I would often try this little game on her, and see her continue smiling and gurgling softly even in her sleep.

I flip through the old album, searching for a picture of her in that blue frock … I don't find one anywhere.

> good ol' tumbler
> I wrap my hands around
> warm coffee

All That's Left

The cow dung paste caressingly patted in her hands and slapped across the outside walls to dry in the scorching Chennai heat, this mother to seven children then moves on to other chores until the day comes to an end, her tiny corner kept ready for the family's early morning bowl of thin ragi porridge. She rests her tired feet on a stiff cotton pillow, as her body yields to the soft korai grass mat spread on the mud floor.

> the desert ...
> and all that's left, the sky
> with all her stars

We

I look at the four generations of women in the photo, with my perky daughter, animatedly talking even when the photo was being taken ... next to her is my grandmother, whose smile is all that I remember. I wonder whether she was ever allowed to go beyond that ... My mother and I are somewhere in there, trying to hold on to our ground, firmly.

Now my daughter, she airs her views on everything ... but isn't home the place to toss ideas to see how they boomerang before you present them to the world?

> we fail to spot
> the oakleaf butterfly ...
> colours in flight

Temple Ponds and Lotus Pads

Temple visits were a must in my childhood. My mother used to go around the whole temple 12, 18, or even 108 times, and I followed her faithfully for as many rounds as I could. That's her evening walk I used to tell people, feeling very wise. When it rained, the mud floors held puddles with the temple carvings reflected in them.

I loved sitting on the steps of the temple pond, my legs dangling in the water, watching frogs on lotus pads waiting to catch the dragonflies that flitted in and out of my vision. Losing sight of the flying insects, I searched frantically to spot them again, a game that kept me occupied until mother called that it was time to leave.

It has been ages since I visited a temple to pray. The crowds and the commercialization of faith ... things have changed so much now.

in the midst
of this raging sea ...
your voice

Burmese Evacuation, 1942

Mother slipped into another era as she began, saying, "I thought this incident was long forgotten, but I remember it as clearly as if it was yesterday. I was just twelve years old then; it was the Burmese evacuation of 1942. Half a million of the Indian community fled Burma into Assam, mostly on foot. Madras city was also evacuated, with families sent off to their villages while the men stayed in the city to work.

"My mother, who was barely 33, took us, her six children to Thiruvaalangadu and we stayed there for over a year with our grandmother. The cousins also poured in from Madras."

> moonless night
>   the village temple
> flooded with devotees

"In those days families were huge, not like your days," Mother quipped. "It was a fun time, for the war to us was too distant and of no immediate concern. Now, when I look back at World War II, it seems so ominous and scary and how I went through that war in my own innocent way is intriguing." Mother smiled, but to me it seemed like she was dazed by the magnitude of this thought.

> how the earth
> bears the beating ...
> delayed rains

Misty Morning

mustard flowers yellow the trodden path back to spring

I row the boat ... my travelling companions come and go, on and off. Parents, siblings, husband, children, friends, Beatles, Kumarji, raga music, haiku ... like the faraway moon, warm and constant on its ever-ending journey, my days wax and wane.

As dense mist passes by, some knock on the door of my boat house and others just barge in to fill my each breath with their thoughts. From this maze I walk out, spinning insults, wounds and rounds of applause into flowers and fruits. Gathering or trying to gather all parts of me into one — whole and undivided.

her low deep moan
fills the misty morning ...
a cow in labour

Moondram Pirai
— The Third Day Moon

My mother would want us to find the third-day moon. "It's most auspicious to see it," she'd insist. Every month this ritual would be followed most religiously. Only on the third day the moon becomes visible to the human eye, as a faint half circle. We would clamour and shout, our fingers pointing here and there, imagining that elusive silver line to be all over the sky.

When my kids were young, not once did I show them or ask them to search for the moondram pirai. Why was that? Maybe in a Mumbai flat one doesn't go searching for a non-existent moon from window to window. Had I become so westernized in my thinking that all the Indian values I grew up on had lost their significance? Most likely, while looking after two kids, I lost touch with nature for a short while …

> the raga blooms
> as he lengthens the note
> pin-drop silence

Into the Future

> the leaves
> never tire of dancing
> spring breeze

The soothsayer with his parrot prepares his show under a banyan tree very close to a mall. People throng around him ... curious children, mothers with huge shopping bags. He meticulously takes out the tiny books and lines them up in front ... pats his parrot as she peeps out of her cage, gives her a red chilli telling her to do a good job. He smiles at the passersby.

> Sunday special:
> the paper boys fresh
> with new stories

A lucky day indeed, for by noon around 13 people have had their future forecast. All of them return with a smile. He has learnt to tell only good things. There was a time when he used to tell the truth, but people frowned and word passed around fast that the soothsayer outside the mall had a foul mouth and his parrot a nasty mind! He likes being truthful, but he loves money more, so he starts to sing a different tune ... a tune that people want to hear.

> talk of kismet —
> eyes on the client's
> bulging wallet

The Missing Game

"Drawing time, children!" I clap my hands. I've taught myself to talk less and be more animated. "Do you hear me?" I gesture wildly. Some are crying and some are eating ... Now, is there a fight over a chair? But why? There are enough chairs for everybody.

> night walk ...
>   the wind scatters
> the fallen leaves

One child is shouting that he doesn't want his apple, orange.

What?

Oh ... With a blue crayon in hand, he says, "Oranges needn't be orange ... don't you see, Miss?"

I see ...

> pillar roots
> supporting the banyan tree
> allow the leaves to be

The Swing

Come rain, sun or moody weather, Grandfather hardly ever missed his walk. As the old kitchen clock struck seven in the morning, he would be tying his shoes and then strut downstairs towards the park. To me, grandfather was always grandfather, always old.

He's been bedridden for the past three months. As I enter his room, he looks up and winks, this man who could never wink 'properly', however many times we tried to teach him. And now, much to my child-like amusement, he blinks both his eyes, his smile running into the creases on his face ...

> the swing: the sky
> of a thousand dreams,
> pulls me in

Heirloom

When I lived at home, coffee percolators were unknown in Chennai. We had lovely filtered coffee made from an ordinary two-cylinder stainless steel container. The top had perforated holes on which we added the freshly roasted and ground South Indian coffee powder. Then we'd top it gently with boiling water, and in a matter of five minutes the decoction would be ready, filling the whole kitchen with the most pleasing aroma the world has ever known!

Seems simple enough! But this happened once in a blue moon. Very often our coffee filter would fail to perform this simple task, much to my mother's dismay. The hot water would bypass the coffee powder, and a rundown brown coloured liquid would be the result. Or the hot water would trickle down at its own pace, almost as if it had a will of its own!

Mother's old coffee filter now rests on my kitchen table. An heirloom treasure, getting more precious with each passing year ...

And as I master the art of making that perfect cuppa coffee, I relive the warmth and aromas of her kitchen.

> receding wave ...
> crab holes breathe
> the milky way

Autumn Note

I remember the shehnai. I remember him. Ustad Bismillah Khan — the maestro. Why, even my kids, who were so young then, remember him. The applause he received for playing the same thing he had played for years. "Some things one can never get tired of," my mother used to say.

That day on the dais, when his son began to play the shehnai — a reed/wind instrument like the flute — the Ustad, with his usual smile running into all the crevices on his face, held his hand high. His poor son had to hold on to a top note, steady — a seeming eternity — until his father's hand came down.

autumn note ... *
his breath holds even
the song's silence

Notes:
* autumn note : in my view means a musical note which is perfect in its musical quality and emotional content.

An Old Song

As kids we learned addition and subtraction by counting the kinds of trees in our backyard and the fruits in each. Those squirrels running up and down ... the coconut, mango and banana trees were so much a part and parcel of the stories we concocted.

It's my father's 90th birthday and I'm back home for the celebration. Our maid, who has been with my parents for more than 25 years, announces that it's time to cut the bananas she has reserved for this family get-together. One branch holds more than 100 bananas — dozens and dozens neatly stacked. For days this raw vegetable is the flavour of all our meals! It's either banana dry curry, bananas in gravy, rice with spiced bananas, mildly salted crisp banana chips ... the list seems endless.

> blossoms sway
> an old song breathes
> through my mind

Afterglow

Unending rains, the hills are green all over. In my balcony, the champa is soaked in fragrance, her edges frayed.

I dread the monsoon slush — my each step grounded in the grip of my flip-flops. Even more, I dread to be on roads that run past me ...

I'm housebound I am.

Period.

Just for a while, the caged mind begins to rake up pleasant memories, then stealthily steps on those sunken ruts. Headlong I'm thrown into the unfathomable depths of old hurts and wounds, and then those soothing licks that heal, sort of ...

the talking inward poet weaves in and out of breath

    afterglow ...
    the old basement clock
    strikes the hour again

Arranged Marriage

Tens of thousands of thirsty throats and more ... dry wells, bore wells go deeper and deeper to find that missing elixir of life ... water. Villages in Chennai this summer went dry.

Colourful saris, glass and gold bangles dwarfed by multicoloured plastic pots. I see muddy street after muddy street with dried-up water tanks ...

By 2 pm, people line up their colourful plastic pots in long serpentine queues and sit down to wait ... for the Government water vehicles to arrive.

    afternoon heat
    women lap up spicy gossip
    steaming hot

Soon teashops open, men assemble straight from work. There is talk of government, politics, sports, regional movies — of Aishwarya Rai, Sania Mirza and A. R. Rehman's Bombay dreams — a runaway success in London ...

Grandparents finding their homes too quiet start walking towards these get-togethers with a purpose. People know each other by their first names; they exchange problems for problems, recipes for jokes ...

    conspiracy —
        moms busy knitting
    their wards in wedlock

caught unaware —
the thickness of rain
on the road

I see her pack the bare minimum ... "I don't need more, Ma," she says emphatically. "I need to carry that load, you understand?"

It's a Himalayan trek of 12 days — you need to take some medicines — some energy food. What do you think the organizers will provide?

She keeps packing — almost nothing.

I get a call from her from the base camp at Kulu Manali. In spite of a bad connection, I can sense her excitement. She's at 4,500 feet. "It's tough; I hope I have the will-power," she says haltingly.

Next, she calls from 11,000 feet. "Ma, I'm holding snow in my hands."

"Ho!" She says casually, "It's just like our freezer box!"

She calls from 13,500 feet. "Ma, we've reached Saurkundi Pass. From here I can see the highest peak of the Himalayas. I've climbed 13,500 feet above sea level, Ma. It's snow everywhere."

She calls from 8,000 feet. "Ma, we slid down the snow. It was such fun that five of us climbed up again to slide down once more!"

I see the great Himalaya through her eyes.

> mango moon —
> a squirrel's half eaten fruit
> nestles in the earth

The Threshold

> distant rapids …
>   a rumbling song
> from the bridge

"Suicide point," the guide says, "you need to see it, Memsahib."
The driver takes the car up the mountain range, without grace
or expertise — it looks like he'll murder us even before we
reach this point. Up and up we go along raw muddy roads.
The car comes mercifully to a halt. We walk toward the famed
suicide point and look ...

Down.
Sheer fall.
A single sheet of dripping mist almost pulls the sky into the
valley. And from beyond the horizon a reddish-orange glow
softly spreads ... the beginnings of another day.

> sudden rain
> bringing to life
> the child in me

Coffee Blossom

"I am constantly bringing things up," I tell my doctor.

"This sounds like heartburn," she says. "The symptoms can be a burning sensation rising in your throat; it can make you sit up at 3 am, maybe with a bout of coughing. Some experience the urge to throw up, with pain and nausea."

I squirm in my plastic chair. "Yes, those are exactly my symptoms."

I pay her hefty fee, take the prescription and walk home ... I don't tell her it has to do with my battle with words. How can I?

> distant horizon
> from wet earth the rise
> of coffee blossoms

The Moon's Company

Every year my parents perform the ceremony of my grandparents' deaths, known as 'Sraaddha.' It is 'a day of remembrance.' Most Hindu families observe this traditional practice to show their respect and heartfelt gratitude to their parents, on the day they died. A Brahmin priest comes over to perform the sraaddha, which is a prayer service, recited in Sanskrit. It takes three to four hours and a special meal is cooked. A ball of rice, called the 'pinda,' which is symbolically meant for the deceased parent and his or her ancestors, is first offered to the crows.

On my recent visit home, my parents were recalling the date when my father's father had passed away. Was it the first half of the waxing or the latter half of the waning of the moon? Father said, "I distinctly remember the full moon giving me company through the long drive to my village on the night my father died."

> open veranda
> warmth of the winter sun
> in each tile

An Hour Passes

> dead body ...
> only the shadows of leaves
> dance on her face

My wife died — thirteen days ago.
To be single again — it's a strange feeling that after sixty-six years of togetherness, I am all alone.

Like the River Cauvery that swells in the monsoons then becomes so thin that it seems almost like a drawn line, my family was huge once, when my five children were small — kids grow wings and take off, and slowly my wife and I just grew accustomed to being by ourselves.

My son and my daughter-in-law are here. They keep insisting that I will feel miserable in London. I keep telling them that I am ready to go with them. My daughter-in-law says "But papa, you have your temple, your friends here. What will you do there? It's a foreign country papa, try to understand."

How can I tell her that I am scared of staying alone? Won't my grandchildren laugh at me?

> sultry morning
> the chameleon changes
> its colours

The Knot Remains

coming of frost
          an old scar
starts to itch

"Where was I? Do not interrupt me, young man ... I lose the thread. Ho! That reminds me of a couplet by Raheem,

Do not cut the thread of love impulsively, once broken it cannot be mended, and even if mended, the knot still remains.

"What a beautiful thought ... ha! Yes, coming back to my story, I told my wife that we should buy a flat in one of those housing schemes for senior citizens. Had we moved in there, I would have made my own friends by now — people my own age. And we could all sit and discuss the present generation, which is a 'gone generation.' For nothing at all they worry. For everything they fuss. If a child fails in nursery — ho ho ho! You tell me, how can a child fail in nursery?"

He beats his thigh boisterously.

"Now hear this, I read it long back somewhere, I forget where — *Old age looks back. Youth looks forward. Middle age looks worried.* Laugh, young man! Where is your sense of humour? The biggest fault of mine was that I listened to my wife too much. I should have put my foot down and booked that flat for seniors. Now, see my predicament? My children don't want me.

Look at the word daughter-in-law closely. Only by law, she is my daughter. 'Law' means force. In force, can there be love ..."

> leafless tree
> the sun rises
> with a walking stick

"Tell me what course to take. What is your profession? A lawyer, you said? Very good! Oh! You have to leave? Yes, I know I've taken a lot of your time. It was a pleasure discussing things with you. I can tell you are a brilliant lawyer. You have my blessings for a bright future."

I take his leave and head for the comfort of my home, two children and a dog ...

> a peepal tree
> abuts a roadside temple
> I think of Buddha

Layers

> zazen hour ...
> I slip into the next
> layer of silence

She's a Buddhist monk and the way she moves around shows her to be one with the discipline of just being. From the teapot she pours the tea, a little at a time into each of the three cups — I see them fill but I'm curious why she doesn't fill the cup at one go. I ask her. She says, "so the strength and warmth are the same in each cup and all of us can enjoy good tea."

> desert wind
> sand fills up the pockets
> of camels' footprints

As I walk back home I remember a story I read a long time ago. Mullah Nasruddin is sitting one evening under an old banyan tree in the village square, plucking the strings of the sitar. Gradually, as expected, a circle of friends gathers around him. He keeps on strumming just one note.

Finally, one villager musters enough courage to inquire, "That's a very nice note you are playing, Mullah, but most of the musicians use all the notes. Why don't you?"

"They are still searching for the note," says the Mullah calmly, "I have found it."

    razor's edge
    a caterpillar's reach
    to the next leaf

The Blue Jacaranda

> waiting for a call
> > that never came ...
> new year's eve

I was your maid. You remember me? The one who used to tie your shoelaces and make the chapathis and that potato curry for you. Pack your lunch and escort you to the bus stop.

The school bus would come to our street corner somewhere around 8 am daily.

Your smile, as you waved goodbye, asking me to be there waiting when you get home in the evening. You had a loud voice.

In case you feel like seeing me, do come over. I stay at The Jacaranda Old-age Ashram. No 18, Queen's Lane, Pune-411009.

Ask for Shalini bai.

Everybody here knows me well and they know you too. I keep talking about you to all the inmates. I posted a similar card to you a year back, but I'm thinking it didn't reach you ...

> restless night ...
> turning and tossing
> the repeat
> > mindsong
> as the ache sinks deeper

LOC

> new year begins
> the firing across borders ...
> old questions

Mother looks up, pain in her eyes. The papers are full of the bomb blasts. She asks, "Can there be something like a 'delete' button in our minds?"

> flowing river ...
>   she recalls
> India's partition

Three months back I had been to Gulmarg, in Kashmir. Most of us were seeing snow for the first time. We made snowballs and threw them at each other like children. Later, we walked towards the Line of Control which was on the adjoining mountain. A row of trees was all we could see but the Gurkha told us that beyond those trees lies the LOC.

Back home, I wonder - did I expect the line to be marked by a fence, a mini wall? And what about borders that arise within our own minds?

> a question
> with many answers ...
> falling blossom

My Springboard

One spring day at twilight, I was walking down the hill path with an elderly gentleman. Shall I call him ... my poet friend, my springboard? He is an old acquaintance of mine, and we would wave or smile at each other on our usual evening walk, around the hill that we share with Pune university.

The day before yesterday, I saw him watering the trees on the hill — Pune is really dry now and as summer nears, it gets worse.

I offered to help water the young saplings we'd planted a year back, aiming for a green hill. As I was talking to him about what makes or breaks a haiku, he said, "Have you read Iqbal, the poet philosopher of Pakistan? I know him from the time when India and Pakistan were one."

With impeccable Urdu pronunciation and a natural throw of head, hands and voice, he recited the poem and even translated it for me.

Beauty asks of Almighty, *why didn't you make me eternal? To which Almighty answers that life is a movie theatre, and it has to move on — the truth of evolution. The moon hearing this, repeats it to the morning star, and the morning star tells it to the dewdrop, which in turn whispers it to a flower and the flower on hearing it, dies.*

raat ki rani ... *
her fragrance rides
the breeze

The next evening, on entering the gate to the university hill, I heard my poet-friend say that there will be no watering the saplings today, as there was no water in the tank ... so walking up the hill he asked, "Do you know why a flower has petals?" He said, "Think, and think." Then smilingly he said that he would recite Ghalib for me, a very delicate poem on why a flower has petals.

The bulbul — India's nightingale — was wailing loudly for spring blossoms. Even the plants far away could hear it, for the bulbul's wail almost filled the cosmic space. The buds, feeling heart-broken, split into petals.

Wah! Is all I could muster ...

Last evening, after half an hour of watering, we took a small break, and I recited a haiku of mine to my poet-friend,

darting fish-like
seven months of life
in my womb

He spontaneously quoted Ghalib in chaste Urdu ... his clear voice rising above the birdcalls. He said, *the wind as you know is flirtatious, here and there, touching, feeling everything as it moves. On a spring morning the wind sees a beautiful blossom and goes towards her, attracted by her beauty, he goes deeper into her solitude and as the wind whizzes past, the blossom elated, in full fragrance, proclaims to the world at large that she has lost her virginity to the wind.*

My poet-friend continues with Ghalib ...

My beloved promised that she would come, the news made me so joyous, given that moment I would have happily died, but deep within my heart, something told me that ultimately she won't come, and that is the reason why you see me alive today.

> howling wind —
> his bamboo flute holds
> an autumn note

Notes:
* raat ki rani : (literally, queen of the night) night jasmine, which blooms at night then dies early in the morning.

The Twist

"This still smells new!" my son-in-law comments, when he gets into my one-year-old car. I take it as a compliment, for I do maintain things well — but on his next visit, he gets me two car fresheners.

> banjo night
> notes spin around
> the dancer

A Level Ground

as the sun dips into the horizon shadows slip away on a breath
of fresh air I begin to whistle a tune

> a night of stars
>> my soul
>>> all over the place

ENDNOTES

1. "The Moving Finger," Omar Khayyam, *Rubaiyat of Omar Khayyam,* Tr. Edward Fitzgerald, Quality Paperback Book Club, 1996.

2. "Trees are poems," Kahlil Gibran, *Kahlil Gibran Ultimate Collection: 21 Books in One Volume*, e-artnow, 9 November 2015.

3. "Thirty spokes," Lao Tzu, *Tao Te Ching,* Tr. Gia-fu Feng and Jane English, Vintage Books, 1989. Page 13

4. "You go around bent!" Kabir, *The Bijak of Kabir,* Tr. Linda Hess and Shukdev Singh, Motilal Banarsidass, 1983.

5. "We are animal," Jay Griffiths, *Wild: An Elemental Journey,* Tarcher 2006.

Poet and editor Kala Ramesh writes and teaches haiku, tanka, haibun and renku to children, undergrads and senior citizens. An external faculty member of the Symbiosis International University Pune since 2012, she teaches Japanese short forms of poetry to undergrads — a first in her country.

Passionate about taking haiku to everyday spaces, Kala initiated the 'HaikuWALL India' project, which invites graffiti artists to paint haiku on city walls. Starting in 2006, she has organised five haiku festivals in India so far. Her love for haiku and her many initiatives culminated in the formation of 'IN Haiku' in 2013 — bringing Indian haiku poets under one umbrella to promote, enjoy, and sink deeper into the beauty and intricacies of haiku and allied Japanese short forms of poetry.

In collaboration with artists, musicians, and dancers, Kala has given several readings in public places. She created the '*Rasika*' form, an eight-verse renku (collaborative linked verses) fashioned after Matsuo Basho's non-thematic style.

Kala is Editor at *Under the Basho* (USA); Editor of the Youth Corner, *Cattails* (USA); Ex-poetry Editor of *Katha.org* (Delhi); Editor of Haiku and Short Verses, *Muse India* (Hyderabad); Deputy Editor-in-Chief, *World Haiku Review* (UK) and serves on the editorial team of *Living Haiku Anthology* and *Living Senryu Anthology* (USA).

Kala's publications include:

Haiku & My Haiku Moments: an Activity Book for Young Haiku Lovers, published by Katha 2010. Awarded the Honourable Mention for Best Book for Children in The Haiku Society of America - Merit Book Awards for 2011.

FIRST Katha eBook of Haiku, Haibun, Senryu and Tanka published by Katha. Editors, Kala Ramesh et al. 2013.

one-line twos, in collaboration with Marlene Mountain, an eBook published by Bones, Denmark 2016.

Editor-in-Chief of *Naad Anunaad: an Anthology of Contemporary World Haiku,* published in 2016 by Vishwakarma Publications. It won the first prize in the anthology section of The Haiku Society of America Merit Book Awards 2017.

the unseen arc, Kala's tanka collection, winner of the Snapshot Press eChapbook Award, UK, June 2017.

Prabha Mallya is an editorial illustrator and comics creator, with a focus on wildlife, natural history and conservation, with regular forays into speculative dystopic futures and Internet culture-inspired modern-day hypotheticals. She has illustrated for *The Wildings, Beastly Tales from Here and There* and *The Jungle Books,* and has created graphic stories for several comics anthologies.

Link to her work: fishkitty.tumblr.com

Printed in Great Britain
by Amazon

50732217R00123